ustr   d

For Dawn, who has a curly plant

First published in 2006 in Great Britain by
Barrington Stoke Ltd
18 Walker Street, Edinburgh, EH3 7LP

www.barringtonstoke.co.uk

This edition first published 2012

ISBN: 978-1-78112-075-0

Printed in China by Leo

Contents

1   A Meeting in the Road   1

2   A Short Visit Home   20

3   The Plant Show Tent   29

4   All the Fun of the Fair   38

5   The Competition   47

6   Later   64

Chapter 1
A Meeting in the Road

One breezy Saturday morning, Pinchton Primm came staggering back from the library with two huge carrier bags full of books about jungles.

My Thoughts About The Rainforest. That was the title of his homework essay. But Pinchton had no thoughts. His brain was a blank because he had nodded off when they had talked about it in class.

The handles of the bags were slicing his fingers in half, but he hoped it would be worth it. If he copied from the books, he wouldn't have to come up with a single *word* of his own, let alone a whole load of thoughts. Pinchton was fed-up. He didn't like having to do any thinking on Saturday mornings. All he wanted was to play on his Xbox without having to think at all. He wanted to lie on his bed with the curtains shut. Sadly, his parents had other plans for him.

He had nearly reached his house (Number 15, Tidy Street, with the smart front garden) when he saw a bush walking towards him.

Startled, he put his bags down and cleaned his glasses on his blazer. He looked again.

It wasn't a bush after all. It was Otterly Weird, dressed in green and carrying the House Plant.

The Weird family had moved in to Number 17, next door (with the awful front garden) just a few months ago. There were eight of them. Maybe nine. There was:

Gran Weird
(Dwarf)

Mrs Weird
(Stunt Woman)

Mr Weird
(Inventor)

Oliver Weird
(Big Brother)

Otterly Weird
(Ott)

Frankly Weird
(The Baby)

Ginger   and   The House
(The Black Cat)   Plant(!)

There was also a strange Thudding Thing
that lived somewhere deep in the house and
acted up whenever anyone came to the door.
Pinchton still hadn't found out what *that* was.
But he kept trying.

Unlike Pinchton, who had to dress in a tidy,
proper way, Ott liked fancy clothes. Pinchton
could see that today was a green day. She wore
green wellingtons, a green dress and a green
cardigan with frog buttons. Over one arm was
a green plastic handbag. On her head was a
Robin Hood hat which had come free with the
cornflakes. (Pinchton knew. He'd had one before

his mother had thrown it away, saying it was silly.)

The House Plant Ott was carrying was also green. It stood up tall in its pot. Its tangled stalks and long thin tendrils twisted about wildly in the wind.

There was something very strange about the House Plant. Not only did it look odd, it was almost as if it – *knew* things. It seemed to listen to what people were saying. It *swayed* at you. It was more like a pet than a plant. Pinchton had once asked Ott if it had a name. She had said, "Don't be daft. It's a Plant."

Yes, the Plant was Weird all right. But then, so was the entire Weird family. Pinchton knew all about them. If his parents knew what Pinchton knew, they would have a fit. Pinchton's parents liked a tidy life. A life without surprises. No sudden shocks or dramas or dressing up in odd clothes.

"Hello, Ott," said Pinchton, "you're looking green."

"I am, aren't I?" said Ott, cheerfully. "That's because I'm a Greenie." She stopped and rested the House Plant on the wall. "Phew. You're heavy, you are."

That last remark was for the Plant, who continued to swish. Although the wind had dropped.

"You're a *what?*" said Pinchton.

"A Greenie. It's a girl's club. Like the Brownies, but green. I'm going to make some new friends. We wear green uniforms. I haven't got one. But I thought I'd get into the mood of the thing."

"What do you do there?" asked Pinchton.

"Grow stuff, mostly. It's about taking care of the Environment."

"Oh, that," said Pinchton, in a gloomy voice. "We did that last term. They made us clean up a bus shelter. This term we're doing the Rainforest."

"At least it's far away so they can't make you clean it," Ott said helpfully.

"I've got it for homework, though," moaned Pinchton.

"Ask Oliver," said Ott. "He loves doing homework. You'll make his weekend."

"Well, if you put it like *that*," said Pinchton. What a good idea! Suddenly, his Saturday looked a whole lot brighter. Oliver would do a great job. He had written an essay for Pinchton once before. Pinchton had got an A and his teacher had looked at him in a surprised way.

"So you like being a Greenie, do you?" he went on.

"I don't know. I've only just joined. It's run by Green Lizard and Green Turtle. We're into wildlife, ponds and window boxes. We're against litter, dumping and pollution."

"Really?" said Pinchton. "Is that so?"

He stared over her shoulder into the Weirds' front garden, which was a riot of soggy boxes and overflowing bins. A shopping trolley lay on one side. A Harley-Davidson motorbike dripped oil into the stinging nettles.

Ott saw what he was looking at. "I see what you mean," she said. "Oh, well."

"You'll have to clear it up," said Pinchton. "Now you're a *Greenie*."

He hadn't really meant this to sound sarcastic, but that was the way it came out. A bit mean. It was just that he hadn't liked all the *we's*. *We* do this, *we* do that. It made him feel grumpy and left out.

"I will," said Ott, with a shrug. "But first I'm going to the cricket field. There's a Fun Day. The Greenies are running a Potted Plant Show." Ott beamed at the House Plant. "And you're going to win, right?"

The House Plant thrashed about as if it agreed – one hundred per cent. Of course, it could have been the wind.

Except that there wasn't any wind.

"It's quite excited," said Ott. "It doesn't get out much."

"Does your gran know it's out?" asked Pinchton. He looked at the Plant and felt rather uneasy. The House Plant always lived in the kitchen, with Gran and Ginger.

"Of course," said Ott. "It was her idea. It's been a bit droopy lately. She says winning a competition will be good for its self-confidence."

"What do you *mean* by that, exactly?" Pinchton asked, carefully.

"Winning the competition will cheer it up. Make it feel good about itself."

"Look," said Pinchton, "I'm no expert, but even I know plants don't ..." He broke off. The House Plant had gone very still indeed. It was standing bolt upright with a sharp, alert air, almost as if it was listening to what Pinchton was saying. Pinchton decided not to finish that sentence.

"Plants don't what?" said Ott.

"Never mind."

"Anyway," Ott went on, "we made it a Good Luck card. I've got it in my bag. Everyone's signed it. Frankly poured on the glitter. Want to see?"

For a second, Pinchton thought about a family who made Good Luck cards for plants. Then he decided not to think about it any more. He also decided to ignore the fact that the Plant's leaves were now hung all over Ott in a happy, thanks-for-the-lovely-card sort of way. He said, "Maybe later."

"Everyone's coming to see the competition. Dad's invented a camera he wants to try out. Mum was meant to be riding the bike over a canyon today but she's put it off until Monday so that she can come too."

"What about Ginger? Is he coming?"

"He's a cat. Depends on his mood."

Suddenly, Pinchton saw his chance to ask about what really puzzled him. Now was the perfect time.

"What about the Thudding Thing you keep in the house?" he said. "The Thing that makes a fuss every time anyone comes calling? Is *that* coming?"

"Ah. I'm glad you asked me about that. You see ..."

Just then, an ice-cream van went past, playing its tune at top volume. Pinchton couldn't hear a word Ott said. He could see her mouth moving, but all he could hear were the noisy bells of the van.

"... so that's why," ended Ott, as the van vanished around the corner.

The front door of Number 17 opened and Frankly Weird toddled out. He wore a yellow and black stripy jump suit. A broken umbrella was tied to his back with string. On his feet were hamster slippers. He stood on the top step, mouth open, eyes huge. He was pointing and making a buzzing noise.

"ZZZZZZZZ," buzzed Frankly.

Pinchton gave a little sigh. The perfect moment was over and he still hadn't solved the mystery of the Thudding Thing.

"Do you want an ice-cream, Frankly?" asked Ott. "All right, in a minute."

"Hello, Frankly," said Pinchton, in a jolly voice. "Are you a bee?"

Frankly looked at him as though he was mad.

"He's a wasp," said Ott. "Different buzz. Anyway, I think the Plant stands a good chance of winning, don't you?"

Pinchton looked at the Plant. It stood proud and tall in its pot, with an air of quiet confidence.

"Well," he said, "er ... I'm sure there won't be many plants quite like this one."

"Want to come?" invited Ott. "You can help carry it."

Pinchton thought about this. He wouldn't be allowed, not until he had done his homework. Besides, weren't Plant Shows very boring? His mother was mad about gardening. She had won lots of prizes and gave talks with slide shows. Sometimes she asked Pinchton to help her. Made him download pictures of flowers from the computer or look up Latin names in a big, boring book. It wasn't something he looked forward to.

"There's other stuff going on," said Ott. "A bouncy castle and stalls and things."

Still, Pinchton wasn't sure if he should say "yes".

"What?" said Ott. "Aren't you allowed?"

"Of course I'm *allowed*," said Pinchton, a bit stiffly. "I'm *allowed* all right. Why wouldn't I be?"

"What, then?" Ott asked. "Is it one of your Meals or something?"

Meals were not messed about with in the Primm household. Meals meant healthy food eaten at the table, with clean hands. Unlike the Weirds, who helped themselves to chips from newspapers spread on the floor. Except that …

"No," said Pinchton. "My parents are going somewhere. They're going to leave me a watercress salad for my lunch."

"Great! We can eat something at the Fun Day," Ott said. "My treat. Popcorn, ice-cream! Hot dogs!"

"Really?" said Pinchton, hopefully. He wasn't allowed any of those things.

"Of course. Unless watercress salad is what you really *want* ..."

"No," said Pinchton. "I'll come. I'll just drop these books off home first. Er – do you want to come in?"

He hoped she wouldn't. There were cream carpets in Number 15. Wellington boots, mad toddlers and strange, potted life forms were not welcome.

"It's all right," said Ott, kindly. "We'll wait out here."

Chapter 2
A Short Visit Home

"Hellooo?" called Pinchton. He dumped his bags in the hall and flapped his fingers to and fro to stop them feeling numb. "I'm back."

"*Is that you, Pinchton?*" came his mother's voice from upstairs. From the bathroom came the angry buzzing of Mr Primm's electric razor.

"Yes, Mother. I'm back from the library. But I'm off out again. I'm helping someone carry something somewhere."

"You're doing what? Rodney, will you please turn off that razor, I can't hear. Sorry, darling, your father's shaving. Say it again."

"*I'm helpfully helping someone carry something!*" yelled Pinchton. He opened the fridge door, looked sadly at the bags of salad leaves and shut it again. No luck. The Fridge Fairy hadn't filled it with Double Chokko Bikky Creamios since the last time he looked.

"*What?*" shouted his mum again.

"*I'm back!*" howled Pinchton. "*But I'm going out again! Someone needs a hand carrying something and I ...*"

"All right, Pinchton, I'm downstairs now. There's no need to yell," said his mother, from just behind him. She was all dressed up with lipstick on, and earrings in the shape of tiny hanging baskets.

"I was just saying ..." Pinchton began for the fourth time.

"I heard what you said. Who are you helping?"

"Ott from next door."

"Oh. Darling, I'm not sure you should be spending time playing with those Weird children. What about your homework?"

"I'm not playing. I'm being helpful. You've always told me to help whenever I can."

"Not if you've got homework. *Rodney, bring my green shoes when you come down, will you?*"

"*What?*" yelled Mr Primm, from the bathroom.

"*Bring my shoes down!*"

23

"*The blue ones?*"

"*No! Green!*"

"So I'm off then," Pinchton put in quickly. "Won't be long and, oh, by the way I'll have something to eat while I'm out."

He said the last bit quite fast, in the hope his mother wouldn't notice.

"*I can't see your green shoes!*" came his father's voice from upstairs.

"*They're under the bed! The ones with the buckles!* What did you just say, Pinchton?"

"*That's your blue ones!*"

"*They're GREEN!*"

And so it went on.

Pinchton went to the table and wrote a little note. It read, *GONE TO DO GOOD DEED. HAVE KEY. EATING OUT.*

Then he left, before his mother could read it. As he opened the front door, he could hear his parents still shouting at each other.

"*Are my reading glasses up there?*" his mother was yelling.

"*The ones with the wire frames? They're here, in the bedroom,*" his father was shouting back.

"*Those aren't my reading glasses. I mean the ones in the case.*"

"*Which case? The blue one?*"

"*It's green. GREEN …*"

Outside, Ott, Frankly and the House Plant waited on the wall. Frankly had an enormous chocolate ice-cream and he was licking it. Some of it was on his nose and on his hands. With them was Oliver. He was very tall and thin, with thick glasses and inky fingers. You could tell just by looking that he never went outside unless someone made him. He saw Pinchton and burst out, "Ott says you've got the Rainforest. I'll do it!"

"Great!" said Pinchton. "Thanks."

"You're welcome," said Oliver. "Got any maths?"

"No."

"Pity. I love maths. I'll start the essay now."

"Not until you've helped carry the Plant," said Ott. Then she added softly to Pinchton, "Gran's made him come out for air. Don't look so glum, Olly, there'll probably be cake at the Fun Day."

"Really?" said Oliver. He loved cake, Pinchton knew. Wedding cake most of all. He ate it with chips.

"I've been thinking," said Pinchton. "We don't have to carry the Plant. We could use the trolley and wheel it there."

"Good idea," agreed Ott. "And I'll get Greenie points for clearing the front garden at the same time."

Together, they got the trolley upright, brushed off the worst of the leaves and mud, squeezed it past the motorbike and trundled it into the street. Then they carefully set the House Plant in it.

Frankly began breathing hard and held up his arms. Some of his ice-cream dropped onto his hamster slippers. Oliver picked him up by his broken umbrella wings and plonked him down into the trolley, next to the Plant.

Both of them looked thrilled.

Chapter 3
The Plant Show Tent

A big, green tent stood in one corner of the field. The banner over the entrance said, HOME GROWN POTTED PLANT COMPETITION. PRIZES!

Two flustered looking ladies in green uniforms were scuttling around in a sea of pots. They kept stopping to write things on their clipboards. There was a long line of people waiting to hand over their entries.

Three girls stood at the front of the line. One had pigtails, one had big ears and one was short. All three wore the proper Greenie uniform with ties and badges and everything. Each held a pot containing pansies – one blue, one yellow and one pink.

They nudged each other as Pinchton, Ott and Oliver came puffing across the field, pushing the trolley. The House Plant and Frankly bounced merrily up and down. Both had chocolate ice-cream all over them.

"Hi!" said Ott with a big smile to the three Greenies as they joined the line. "Phew! Made it. These are my brothers, Oliver and Frankly, and this is my friend Pinchton." Then she nodded to the three girls. "This is Paula, Betty and Carol."

"Hello," said Oliver. He lifted Frankly out of the trolley and set him on his feet. Frankly took off at once, buzzing loudly. "And goodbye," added Oliver. He walked away towards the cake tent. Pinchton was left with Ott to chat to the three Greenies.

Pinchton needn't have worried. They didn't even look at him. Pigtails (Paula) stared at Ott and said, "It's not fancy dress, you know. Why are you wearing those funny clothes?"

"Why not?" said Ott. "They're green, aren't they?"

"Why haven't you got a proper uniform?" poked in Bat Ears (Betty).

"Does your mother let you go out wearing that?" sneered Shorty (Carol).

"Of course," said Ott, surprised. "Why wouldn't she?"

32

Pinchton thought about Mrs Weird, orange-haired biker stunt woman. She wore pink cowboy boots and wrestled sharks as her job. You could go out wearing swimming trunks with a joke arrow through your head and she wouldn't turn a hair.

"What's *that*?" asked Pigtails, pointing at the House Plant.

For the last few minutes, anyone who had been looking would have seen that the Plant was turning sharply to and fro. It looked as if it was listening with keen interest to everything that was being said. But nobody *had* noticed. And now that the girls turned to look at it, it settled down and looked all innocent. Just like a normal plant growing quietly in its pot.

"Our House Plant," said Ott. She wiped the ice-cream from its stalks with the end of Pinchton's tie.

"It's bald," said Pigtails. "It's got no leaves. Bald and ugly."

"It gives me the creeps," agreed Bat Ears.

"Me, too," piped up Shorty.

"Move on up, girls," called out one of the flustered green ladies. The one with the Green Lizard name badge. "Yes, you, dears, it's your turn. Oh, *pansies*. My favourite. Got your names on the pots? All right, put them down there ... Oh my!" She gave a gasp and clutched at her heart. "What's *that*?"

The House Plant was looking at her, over Ott's shoulder.

"Our House Plant," Ott explained calmly.

"I see," nodded Green Lizard. "And you grew this yourself, did you?"

"*It* grew itself. We just looked after it."

"Well!" said Green Lizard. "I really don't know what to say. Are you quite sure it's home grown? The rules are very strict about that. It's just that it doesn't look like the kind of thing that would grow in England, I don't think I've ever ... Mary! Come here, dear, will you?"

The second flustered green lady came bustling up.

"Have you ever seen anything like this, dear?" asked Green Lizard.

She pointed to the House Plant, who was on its best behaviour. It stood ramrod straight and was trying to look as if it wasn't listening.

"My goodness," said Green Turtle. She sounded nervous. "I really don't think I've ever seen a plant like this before. What is it?"

"I don't know. What is it? Does it have a name?" Green Lizard turned and asked Ott.

"Look …" said Pinchton, suddenly. The sun was shining, he could see a van selling hot dogs and he was getting tired. "Look, what's the problem? It's a potted plant and it grew at home. So we'll just wheel it on into the tent, shall we? Ready, Ott? Push!"

Sometimes, you had to be firm.

Chapter 4
All the Fun of the Fair

"I hope it's all right," said Ott.

Ott and Pinchton were sitting on a bench at the edge of the field eating hotdogs. They could see everything from there. The field was crowded. There were queues for the ice-cream van, the hot dog stall and the clown who made animals from balloons. Further away, they could see children happily jumping on the Bouncy Castle while Frankly stole all their shoes. He already had quite a pile behind a bush.

There was no sign of Oliver. He must still be in the cake tent.

Pinchton had a balloon animal. It was a purple giraffe. He rather liked it. He had also liked the ice-cream. He had very much enjoyed the toffee apple, the candyfloss, the popcorn, the lollies and the fizzy drinks. And, of course, the hot dog. Ott had bought him all those things and Pinchton had loved them all. He just couldn't get enough junk food.

"It'll be getting bored by now," went on Ott. "I warned it to behave, but it's not very good at paying attention for long."

They had left the House Plant on the floor at the back of the plant tent. It was too tall to go on a table. It towered over the pansies that the three Greenie girls had put carefully down on the table. The pansies were arranged in a pretty group. They made the Plant look even more odd but it didn't seem to care.

Ott had tucked the Good Luck card into the earth in its pot. Then she kissed the tips of its tendrils and left with Pinchton following on behind her. That was ages ago.

"Ott?" said Pinchton, as he licked ketchup from his fingers.

"What?"

He had to say it.

"The Plant. There are … things about it that … it seems to be a bit … look, it's *more* than just a plant, isn't it? It's … something else. Isn't it?"

There. It was out. He'd said it.

"Who knows?" said Ott, with a shrug. "It grew from one of Gran's beans. One day it was just a cute little shoot poking up from its pot and now look at it. Try looking in one of your jungle books from the library. Perhaps it's in there."

"I will," said Pinchton. He would, too.

There came a sudden, loud crackling, and a booming voice came over the loud speaker, "LADIES AND GENTLEMEN, THE JUDGING OF THE POTTED PLANT COMPETITION IS ABOUT TO BEGIN. PLEASE MAKE YOUR WAY TO THE GREEN TENT, WHERE ..."

No one heard any more. A motorbike came roaring into the field. The engine cut off and someone dressed all in leather jumped off the bike in a dramatic cloud of blue smoke.

It was Mrs Weird, in her pink cowboy boots.

There was someone else on the bike.
A second person in a dirty white lab coat
clambered off the bike's pillion seat. He stood
blinking around like a mole in daylight. Around
his neck hung an odd-looking black box.

That was Mr Weird, plus home-made
camera.

"Mum and Dad, just in time," said Ott, with
a sigh of relief.

"But where's your gran?" said Pinchton.

"What's that?" came Gran's voice, from
right behind them. Gran did that sort of thing
a lot. It always made Pinchton feel uneasy. He
whirled around and there was Gran, in her
black shawl. She smiled happily up at him.
Ginger the black cat, was twisting around her
neat little black boots. However had they got
there without him seeing?

"So," said Gran, brightly. She smiled at Ott and Pinchton and linked her arms with theirs. "What are we waiting for? Let's go and watch the Plant win."

"How do you know it'll win?" asked Pinchton as they set off across the field.

"Lucky day for Aries," said Gran, with a mysterious wink. She set a lot of store by the stars. Pinchton knew that.

"Hello, chickens," boomed Mrs Weird, as they came up. "Having fun? Where's Frankly?"

"Stealing shoes," said Ott, pointing at the Bouncy Castle in the far corner of the field. There was quite a panic going on. Grown-ups and barefoot children were running around in circles, shouting a lot. Over behind the bush, Pinchton could just see Frankly adding a small red sandal to his pile of shoes.

"That's my baby," said Mrs Weird, fondly. "Look at him, Gran. See how he makes his own fun."

"Makes you proud," agreed Gran. "Where's Oliver?"

"In the cake tent," said Pinchton.

"As long as he's not doing homework," said Mrs Weird.

Pinchton's mouth fell open. Was it possible that such words could come from a mother's mouth?

"Say cheese," cried Mr Weird, suddenly. He lifted the black box up in front of his eyes. There was a whirring, a blinding flash and a sharp, loud bang. Pinchton gave a little scream and jumped. Nobody else did.

Mr Weird blew on his camera, which was smoking a bit.

"That'll be a good one, Dead," said Mrs Weird and beamed at Mr Weird. "A lovely family photo." Was Dad called Dead, then? That couldn't be his name, surely?

"I didn't like that bang," said Mr Weird, shaking his head. "That's not supposed to happen. Too many chillies, perhaps."

Chillies? thought Pinchton. A camera that runs on *chillies*?

They made their way to the big green tent. Oliver came out of the cake tent as they passed by and Mrs Weird went across to scoop up Frankly from the other side of the field.

Time for the show!

Chapter 5
The Competition

The plant tent was crowded. The Plant Show was one of the most important events of the day. To Pinchton's relief, the House Plant was exactly where they had left it – towards the back, on the floor, next to the pansies.

Why did he feel so relieved? He wasn't sure. What had he expected the Plant to do? Hop around in its pot, like in a sack race? Crawl out and walk around? Ridiculous.

The Weirds waved to it as they shuffled past. Oliver gave a thumbs up and Ott blew it a kiss. Mr Weird held up his camera and looked at it through the view finder. The Plant was very good. It stayed still and plant-like. But as Pinchton went by, he thought he saw its very top tendril give a little flicker. Almost like a wink.

Green Lizard and Green Turtle had done a good job of sorting all the plants out. The pots were set out on trestle tables, along two sides of the tent. There were spiky plants and leafy ones. Some had flowers, some didn't. Some were tiny, some were big. But none of them was as big or as strange as the House Plant.

Between the two tables was a walkway for the judge. At the far end of the tent there was a small table set with a white cloth and three silver cups. The onlookers stood in the middle of the tent, behind some ropes.

The crowds moved out of the way as the Weirds went up to the front, by the ropes. Gran was first. Frankly rode on Mrs Weird's shoulders. He was waving the little red sandal he'd found and his broken umbrella wasp wings flapped around as people dodged out of his way. Next came Oliver, licking icing sugar from his fingers and staring at the ceiling. Pinchton thought he was doing hard sums in his head. Ott held on to Mr Weird, who was still fiddling with his camera.

They looked very odd. A lot of people turned round and stared at them. Pinchton shuffled along behind them all. At least, *he* looked normal. The three Greenie girls looked over to him and made faces. He ignored them, and felt very good about that.

When Pinchton got to the front, he saw his reflection in the biggest silver cup. He didn't look normal at all! His tie was all crooked, his shirt was covered in ice-cream and there were

ketchup stains on his blazer. He looked down and saw that a button had come off as well. Plus, the trolley had ripped his trousers. There was a huge, great, flapping hole on his knee. The purple giraffe balloon was beginning to go flat.

He looked awful. There would be big trouble if his mother saw him like this.

"Ahem." Green Lizard was standing in front of the table with the cups. Green Turtle was behind her, next to a tent flap. The crowd went quiet. The judging was about to begin.

"Welcome," said Green Lizard. "Welcome to our annual Potted Plant competition, and this year we have a record number of entries."

"Bravo!" boomed Mrs Weird, and on her shoulders Frankly bounced up and down with excitement and buzzed loudly. Everybody stared.

"I'm delighted to be able to welcome our judge," went on Green Lizard. "Ladies and Gentlemen, our judge this year is local gardening expert – Mrs Edwina Primm."

Green Turtle opened the tent flap and – oh, what a nightmare! Oh, horror!

"It's your mum," said Ott. "Fancy that."

Pinchton should have known, of course. The earrings and the lipstick and the green shoes. His dad getting ratty. It all had to mean his mum had one of her gardening events. Why hadn't he put two and two together?

Mrs Primm gave the crowds a big smile as she looked all round the tent. When she spotted the Weirds, the smile flickered a bit. It froze altogether when she spotted Pinchton. He was standing right in front. She couldn't miss him.

Pinchton felt as if her eyes were drilling into him. He tried to hold the balloon giraffe over the tear in his trousers, but it was no good. He tried to smile and gave a weak little wave.

Mrs Primm looked slowly at his dirty blazer.

"So," Green Lizard went on, "without more ado, we'll begin. The judge will walk around and decide which plant she thinks deserves the title of Best in Show. She will be looking at the soil in the pots to see that the plants have been properly looked after, fed and watered well ..."

There came a tap on Pinchton's back. He turned around. As if things weren't bad enough, there stood his father.

"Hello, Father," said Pinchton, with a long sigh.

"Hello, son," said Mr Primm. He didn't sound too cheerful either. Gardening competitions weren't his idea of the best way to spend Saturday afternoons. "What are you doing here?"

"Oh, you know," said Pinchton, not sure what to say.

"No, I don't," said his father.

"I'm finding out about plants," said Pinchton. "For my homework. And I'm – er … helping Otterly with the House Plant."

He nodded over his shoulder at the Plant.

"Your mother's not very happy," said Mr Primm. "You're very dirty, you know."

"I know," muttered Pinchton.

"I see you've had a hot dog," said his father, as he looked at Pinchton's shirt with its ketchup stains.

"Yes," said Pinchton. "Shall I get *you* one?"

"Better not," said his father, rather sadly. He looked back over at his wife. He knew they were having Sprout Surprise for supper when they got home.

Mrs Primm was now walking down between the plant tables as if she was the Queen. Every now and then she stopped, looked closely at a plant, and bent down to sniff the soil in the pots. Then she would whisper something to Green Lizard and Green Turtle. They listened carefully and made notes on their clipboards.

Every so often she would look quickly over at Pinchton. She would have things to say to him, too. He could tell.

And now she was just beside the table where the Greenies' pansies were.

"What's happening?" hissed Ott. The action was all towards the back of the tent now and she couldn't see. "Has your mum got to our Plant? Does she like it? Can you see?"

"No," said Pinchton.

But he could see. His mother was bending down to inspect the pansies. She was smiling at the pansies. She was impressed, you could tell. She murmured something to Green Lizard and Green Turtle, who nodded and pointed to the three Greenie girls, who looked smug.

And then, Mrs Primm saw the House Plant.

A hush fell on the tent. Everyone waited to see what Mrs Primm would say. A lot of people had seen the House Plant. Well, it was hard to miss. And a lot of them were gardeners. They didn't like to admit that they didn't know what the Plant was. How would the judge react?

"Get a shot of this, Dead," Mrs Weird said. "Another nice pic for the album, eh?"

"I will," agreed Mr Weird. "I think I've fixed the camera now."

Mr Weird began to push through the crowd towards the Plant. He kept shouting, "Excuse me, madam!" and "Begging your pardon, sir!" and waving his camera.

Mrs Primm looked at the House Plant. The House Plant looked at Mrs Primm.

"How's it doing?" begged Ott. "Is it behaving itself?"

"Yes," said Pinchton, "it is."

It was, too. It stood straight, tall and proud. It looked – cool. Pinchton wasn't allowed to be cool, but he knew coolness when he saw it. He felt very proud of the Plant as he saw it there, growing away in its own weird, ugly way and standing up tall among all the normal plants. Pinchton almost had tears in his eyes.

Almost. Hey, come on, he wasn't that wet. Weeping over a plant? Please.

But he felt sorry it couldn't win. And it couldn't. He knew that the moment he saw the look on his mother's face. Ott would be disappointed. What Gran had seen in the stars for today would be wrong. What an anti-climax to a happy day out.

His mother and her Greenie helpers whispered together. Then they shook their heads and began to make grim marks on their clipboards.

Suddenly, someone shouted, "Smile, please!" It was a voice Pinchton knew.

There was a violent flash, followed by another sharp bang, as Mr Weird took another photograph. Mrs Primm gave a startled scream and clutched at Green Lizard and Green Turtle.

"Sorry," called Mr Weird, from the centre of a black smoke cloud. "Teething troubles with the camera."

Blinking and looking rather shaken, Mrs Primm wobbled her way back between the tables to the judge's chair. She flopped down with a sigh of relief. It was all too much – seeing Pinchton, coming right up close to a new plant life form and having her photograph taken by an exploding camera. All that, plus painful shoes.

"The judge has chosen the winners," Green Lizard said loudly. "In third place, we have Mr Mole's rubber plant."

A small, smiling man scuttled up and Mrs Primm stood up to give him the smallest silver cup. Everyone clapped politely.

"In second place is Mrs Wilkinson's fern," went on Green Lizard. A lady with round rosy cheeks gave a delighted cry and hurried forward. She got the middle-sized cup from Mrs Primm.

"And the joint winners of this year's competition," said Green Lizard, and she gave an enormous smile, "are the delightful pots of pansies, from our very own ..."

A sudden, terrible scream rang out. Everyone turned. Pigtails was pointing in horror at the table where the pansies were. Or where the pansies *had* been.

They were pansies no more. They were stalks. Not a petal was left. It was as if someone had come along with a pair of grass clippers and lopped their heads off.

Cries of shock and surprise rose up from the crowd. Who could have done this terrible deed?

Pinchton knew. He looked over to the House Plant. It still sat in its pot, as if it was the very picture of innocence.

It looked – full.

Chapter 6
Later

A few days later, Pinchton sat in the Weirds' kitchen, eating chips and looking at two photos. He had nipped in to see the Weirds on his way back from school. He had got another A and a handshake from the headmaster for Oliver's Rainforest essay. He had to say thank you.

Ott, Gran and the House Plant were the only people there. Mr Weird was down in the cellar, inventing something else which would explode, like the camera. Mrs Weird was away jumping off high buildings somewhere. Frankly and Ginger were in the garden. Pinchton could see them climbing the big tree. Oliver was in his attic room playing his banjo.

"Good one of you," said Ott, and she pointed at the first photo. In it were Gran, Ginger, Ott and Mrs Weird all smiling away and Pinchton, jumping with shock because the camera had exploded for the first time.

"Hmm," said Pinchton.

"The stains on your blazer have come out really well," said Ott as Pinchton went on looking at the photo.

"They haven't," he said. "Mother's had to have it dry cleaned."

"This is the best photo," went on Ott, "you can see the Plant getting ready to attack. See?"

"Yes," said Pinchton, "I do."

In the second photo, Mrs Primm was staggering backwards. Her eyes were starting out of her head and her mouth was frozen in an O of surprise. And there was the Plant – crouched down behind the pansies, all long and low and hunter-like, with its stalks bunched up.

"Bless," said Gran, with a fond look at the Plant, who was back where it always was, on the table. "Enjoyed yerself, didn't you? Your lucky day."

The Plant swayed in agreement.

"But it didn't win," said Pinchton. "It didn't bring home the cup."

"Nor did the pansies," pointed out Ott. "Nobody won."

That was true. The Plant Show had ended in a terrible muddle. There had been tears, shouting, shocked horror, you name it. Most people thought that some cheating sneak with scissors had chopped off all the pansies' heads when no one was looking. It must have happened when that Weird fellow's camera exploded. Whatever next?

In fact, the truth was quite different and they were looking right at it. But nobody could see it. A Plant eating the competition? Don't talk so daft.

Anyway, there had been a huge fuss. People had shouted at each other and said terrible things. Green Lizard got most upset. The Greenie girls wailed. A grim Mrs Primm had to be helped to the car by Pinchton's father. At one point, a new crowd of furious parents and their small children came sweeping into the tent and sparked off a new row. Something to do with Frankly's shoe stealing game … and then …

Pinchton stopped thinking about it. The memories were too painful. The worst memories were of when they got home at last and his mother started on about the state of his clothes. He had been told off for a very long time and then sent to his room without, how sad, any Sprout Surprise.

But he had spent the evening doing something very useful. He wasn't allowed to go on his PlayStation, so he looked through all his library books to see if he could find out anything about the Plant.

"Poor Plant," went on Ott, "Mum put it in the corner in disgrace. But she took it out again when I told her about Paula and Betty and Carol and how mean they were. It was only getting its own back."

"Quite right, too," agreed Gran. She was cutting up potatoes in record time. "They had it comin' to 'em. You're not to go to the Greenies no more, Ott, you don't need friends like them. Shout up to Oliver, I'm doing more chips."

Ott went out into the hall. At the same time, Gran opened the kitchen door and scuttled into the garden to collect Frankly and Ginger, who were by now far too high up the tree.

Pinchton was left alone with the House Plant.

He reached over and gave one of the nearest stalks a friendly little pinch.

The Plant stretched out a tendril and ruffled his hair.

He hadn't found the Plant in any of the library books. Well, he hadn't expected to. But, to his total amazement, he had found out a whole lot of interesting things. The Rainforest wasn't boring at all. In fact, he'd had fun looking up stuff about it. Maybe next time, he would write his own essay too.

Maybe.

He could hear Ott shouting up the stairs for Oliver. From somewhere in the house, came a mysterious thudding noise followed by a snarl.

What *was* that? He really must find out.

Our books are tested
for children and young people by
children and young people.

Thanks to everyone who consulted on
a manuscript for their time and effort in
helping us to make our books better
for our readers.